CRAZY CONTRAPTIONS
COLOURING BOOK

BOLD MOVE IN THE CAMPAIGN TO DO AWAY WITH RAILWAY PORTERS

THE 'MODESTY' SEASIDE BUNGALOW

CRAZY CONTRAPTIONS
COLOURING BOOK

A WONDERFUL SELECTION
OF INGENIOUS IMAGES

ARCTURUS

Picture credits

ARCTURUS

This edition published in 2015 by Arcturus Publishing Limited
26/27 Bickels Yard, 151–153 Bermondsey Street,
London SE1 3HA

Copyright © Arcturus Holdings Limited

ISBN: 978-1-78404-510-4
AD004454NT

Printed in China

Introduction

The *Crazy Contraptions Colouring Book* features the work of W. Heath Robinson, a cartoonist famed for his distinctive drawings of mind-bogglingly complicated contraptions designed to achieve the simplest of tasks. Heath Robinson's gently humorous take on early 20th-century life encompasses designs for unlikely household gadgets, observations on the vagaries of the British railway system, and extreme measures for securing a suitable wife.

There is a wealth of pictures for you to colour here – from amphibious vehicles and industrial machinery for stretching tripe, to mechanisms which help raise you gracefully from your armchair. There are also some wry, witty scenes which highlight the anxieties of life in wartime.

So get colouring and unleash your own inventive spirit! Who knows where it might lead?

COMMUNAL JOYS IN THE STONE AGE --
THE ORIGIN OF THE ROUNDABOUT

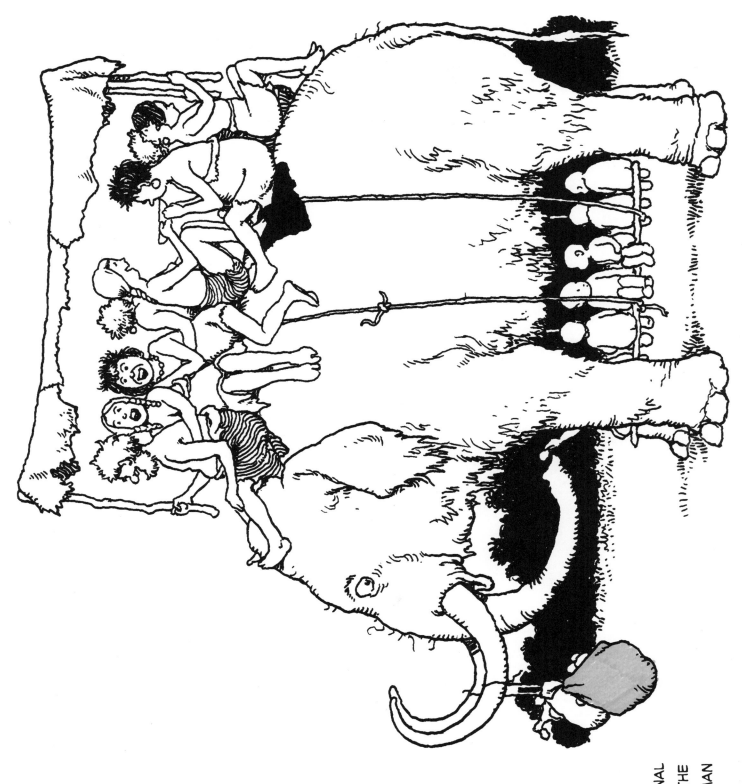

THE COMMUNAL
SPIRIT OF THE
PILTDOWN MAN

EARLY RAILWAY PIONEERS PROSPECTING FOR A SITE FOR A TERMINUS BY THE UPPER
REACHES OF THE PADDINGTON CANAL

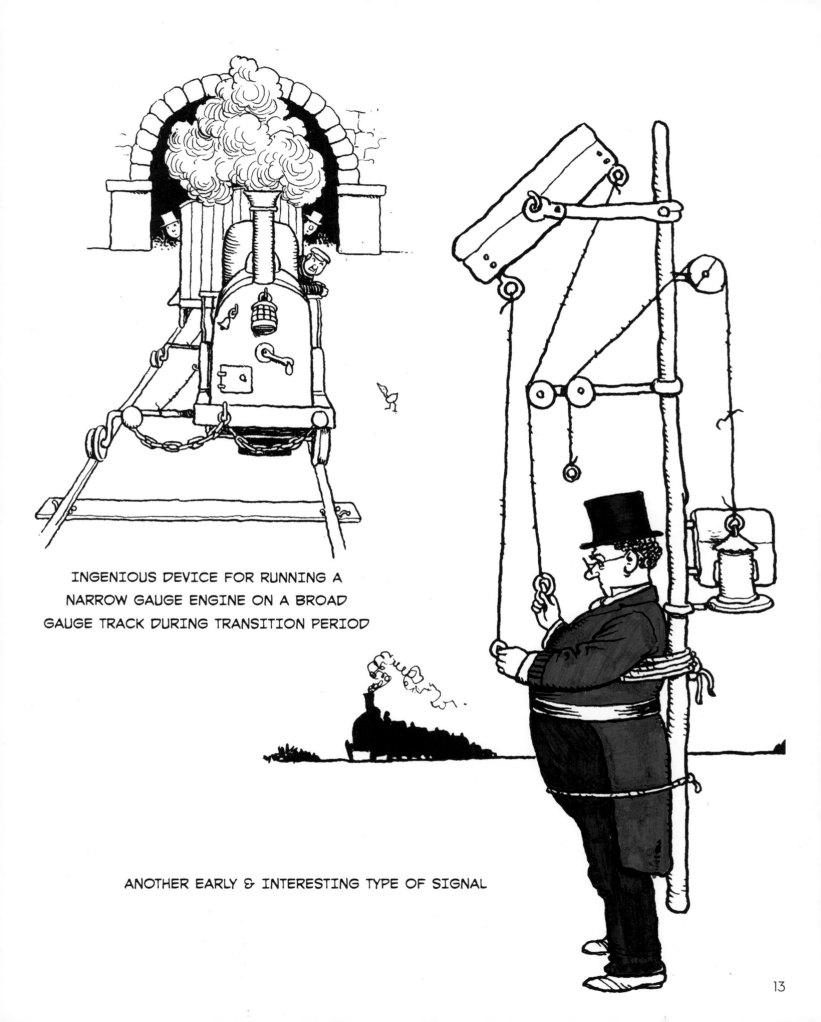

INGENIOUS DEVICE FOR RUNNING A
NARROW GAUGE ENGINE ON A BROAD
GAUGE TRACK DURING TRANSITION PERIOD

ANOTHER EARLY & INTERESTING TYPE OF SIGNAL

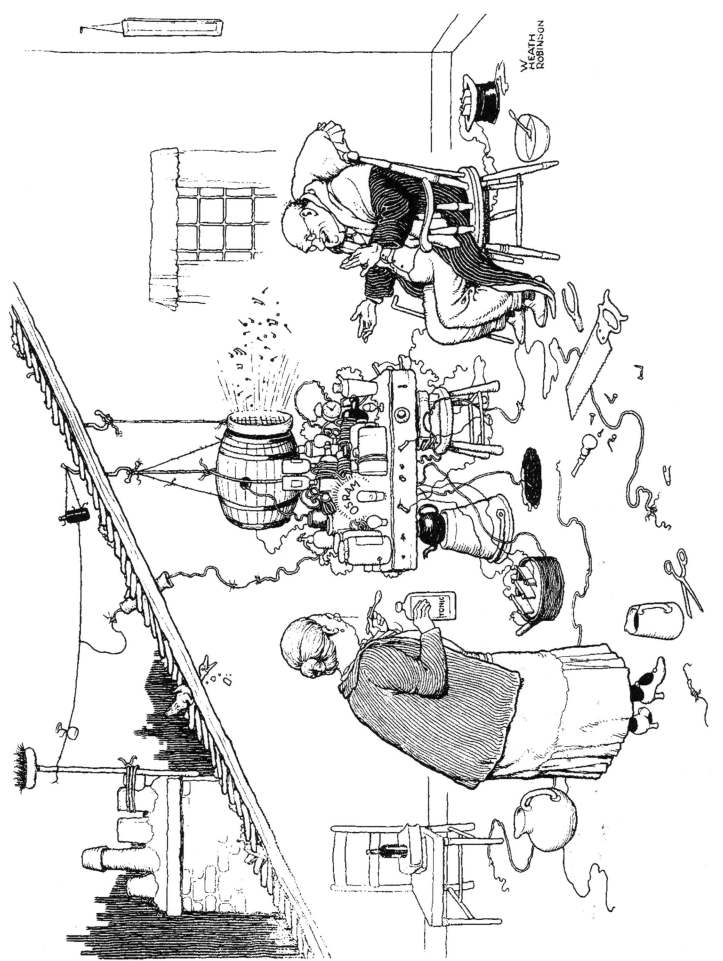

CONTEMPTIBLE PLOT BY THE FIRST LORD AND HIS GANG TO INJECT FLU GERMS INTO
FIELD MARSHAL GOERING BY HYDRAULIC PRESSURE

INGENIOUS PLAN FOR FIXING THE APPROXIMATE TIMES FOR TRAINS TO COVER
THE REQUIRED DISTANCES; USED SUCCESSFULLY IN THE COMPILATION OF THE
FIRST TIMETABLE

A VERY EARLY TYPE OF MECHANICAL SIGNAL NOW RARELY TO BE SEEN

MAGNETIC AIDS TO SKATERS TO BE INSTALLED IN THE LONDON PARKS
DURING THE SKATING SEASON

INSTALLING THE ELECTRIC TELEGRAPH BETWEEN PADDINGTON AND SLOUGH

THE FIRST 'LADIES ONLY' COMPARTMENT

THE HARMONIC
DRESSER FOR
RELIEVING
KITCHEN TOIL

PARLOUR GOLF

HOW THEY NEGOTIATED THE FLOODED DISTRICTS IN THE SHORT CUT TO THE WEST

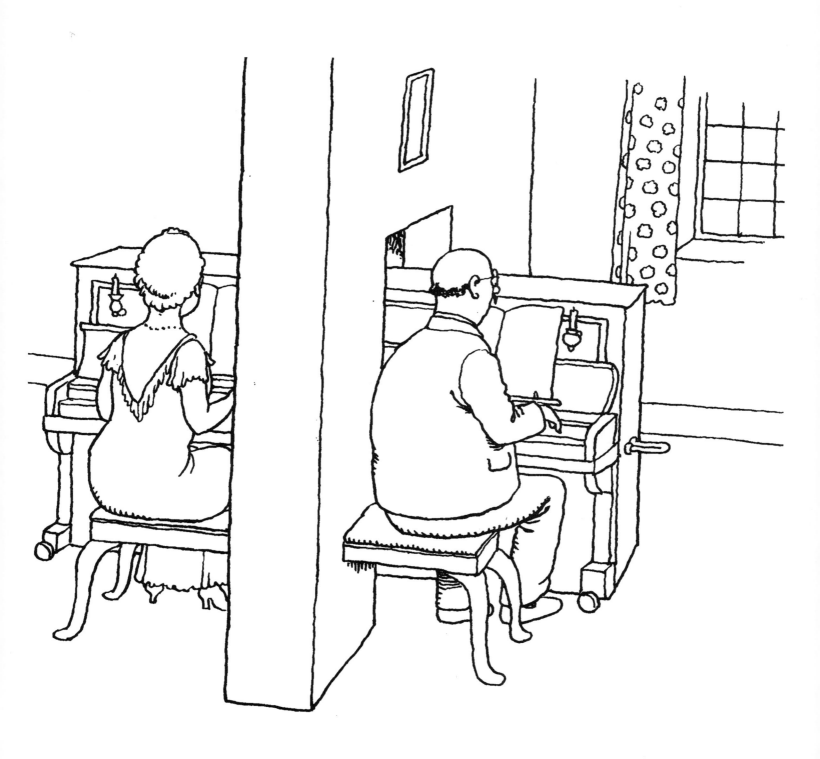

THE COMMUNITY PIANO FOR DUETS WITH NEXT DOOR NEIGHBOURS

MODESTY TOILET BOXES FOR THOSE WHO SHARE A COMMON DRESSING ROOM

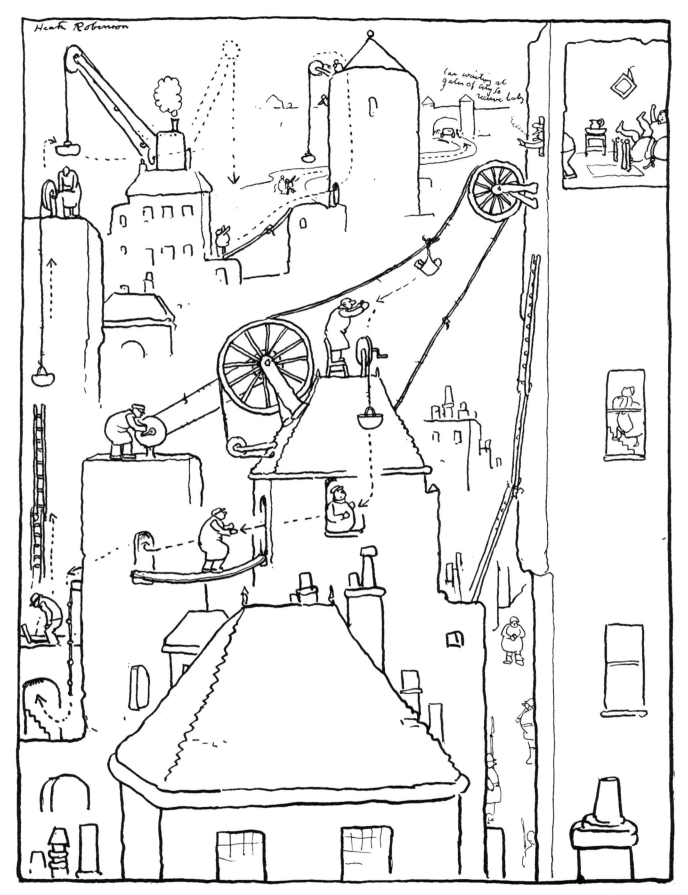

LORD HAW HAW'S LATEST REVELATION --

INHUMAN CONSPIRACY BY THE FIRST LORD OF THE ADMIRALTY TO KIDNAP

GOERING'S BABY

A NEW MACHINE FOR SPEEDING UP THE BREAKFAST
EGG IN A COMMUNAL KITCHEN

ANOTHER GROSS INFRINGEMENT OF THE INTERNATIONAL CODE TO BE ATTRIBUTED TO THE NAZIS --
THE FIRST LORD DISGUISED AS A 'U' BOAT TORPEDOING DUCKS IN KENSINGTON GARDENS

COWARDLY MANOEUVRE BY THE FIRST LORD TO KIDNAP LORD HAW HAW

HOW TO PRESERVE YOUR EGGS WHEN THEY ARE NEW LAID --
GOODALL'S WATER GLASS

A RECENTLY REVISED FORM OF THE AVELING SHUTTLE DUMPER

49

ACCUSTOMING ONESELF TO THE VAGARIES OF OUR CLIMATE IN
A MEDICALLY APPROVED GLASS CABINET

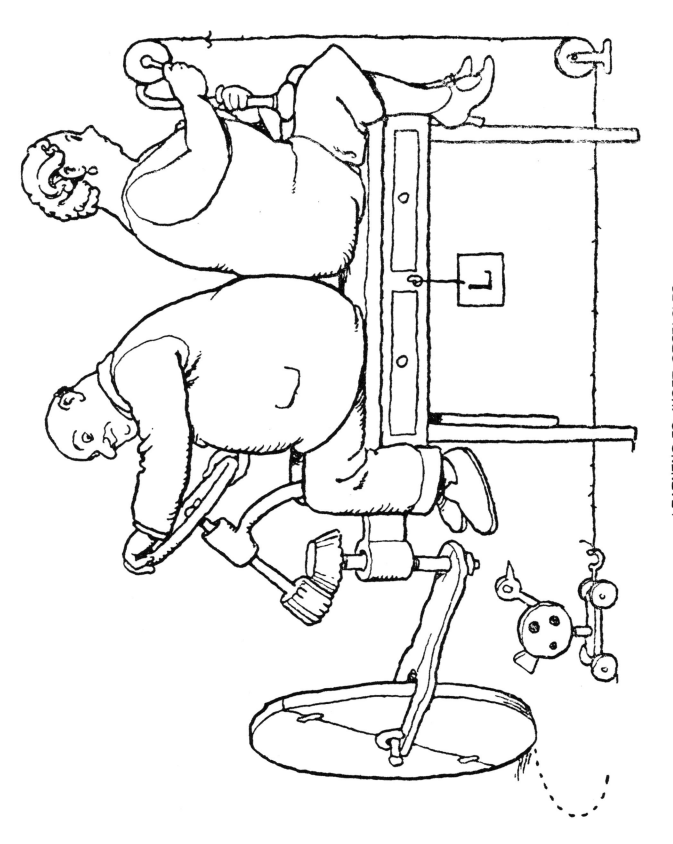

LEARNING TO AVOID OBSTACLES

TEMPORARY MEASURES TO DEAL WITH SHORTAGE OF MATERIALS IN A HAGGIS MILL
IN THE NORTH OF SCOTLAND

THE CHANGE OVER FROM BROAD TO NARROW GAUGE

THE SOUNDNESS OF NEWTON'S LAWS

STRETCHING TRIPE TO INCREASE OUR SUPPLIES IN THE STRETCHING VAULTS
OF AN OLD SMITHFIELD TRIPE WORKS

A LITTLE MECHANICAL HELP IN RISING
GRACEFULLY FROM A LOUNGE CHAIR

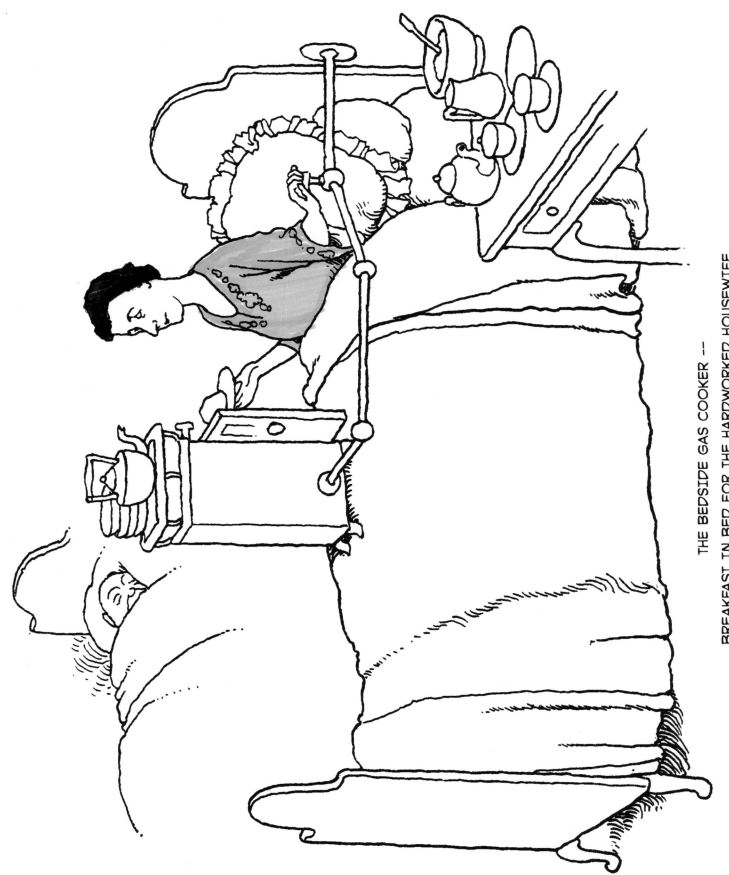

THE BEDSIDE GAS COOKER --

BREAKFAST IN BED FOR THE HARDWORKED HOUSEWIFE

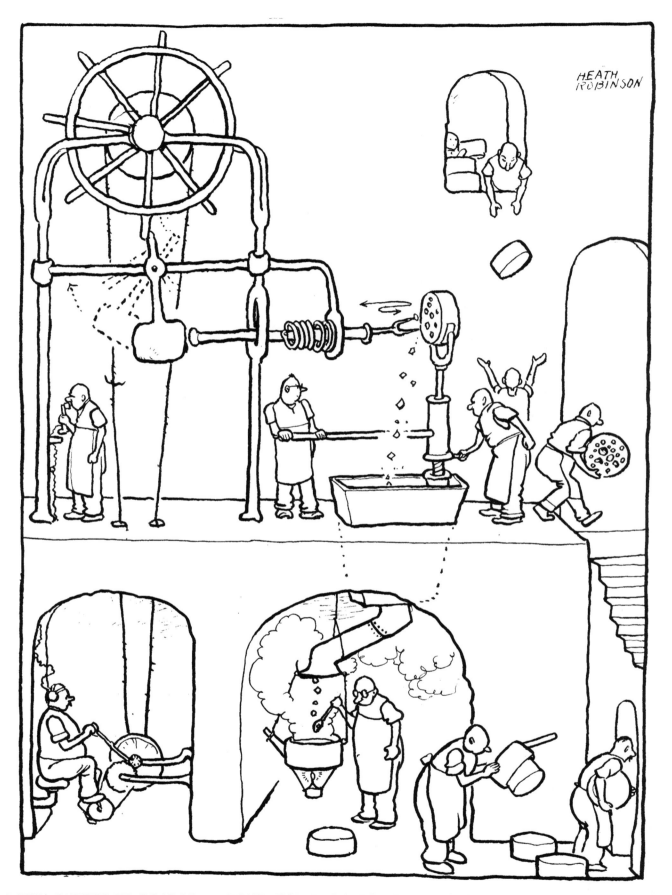

WHEN CHEESE IS SCARCE -- DOUBLING GLOUCESTER CHEESES BY THE GRUYERE METHOD

VARIED DUTIES OF THE RAILWAY POLICE

NEW PLANT IN A MODERN JAM WORKS FOR INCREASING THE SUPPLY OF GREENGAGE JAM

HOME MADE CAR --
EARLY EXERCISE IN STEERING

TESTING THE BATTERY --
HOME MADE CAR

A WELL-THOUGHT-OUT AND NEARLY SUCCESSFUL EXPERIMENT BY EARLY RAILWAY PIONEER

THE AUTOMATIC EGG RATIONER -- FOR WHEN EGGS ARE RATIONED

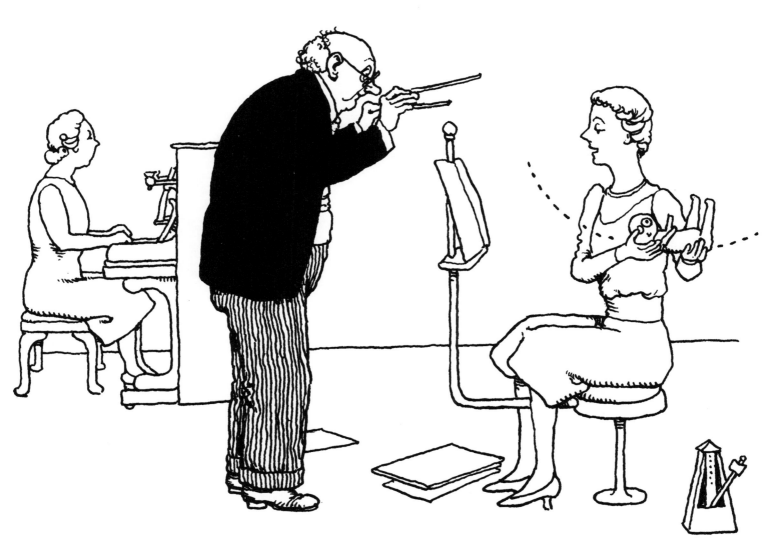

CULTIVATING THE PERFECT LULLABY RHYTHM

THE DRESSER-PIANO

STEAMING THE LODGERS' BREAKFAST KIPPERS

BROWNING SHARPLY AFTER STEAMING

OLD WINDING METHOD

KEEPING THE ROAST CHICKENS WARM WHEN
THE BOARDERS ARE LATE AT THE OFFICE

WARMING UP COLD BOILED EGGS
WITHOUT HARDENING

THE OLD SWING METHOD OF
GRILLING SAUSAGES OVER
THE GAS WITHOUT BURNING

PRIMITIVE METHOD OF STEAMING JOINT,
YORKSHIRE PUDDING, TWO VEGS & SWEET

AN EARLY ATTEMPT AT FUEL
ECONOMY IN DEALING
WITH EGGS & BACON

IN PRE-ROTAPAN DAYS

83

A WASH AND BRUSH-UP AT SWINDON

COURTSHIP -- SYNCHRONISING HEART BEATS

TESTING FIANCÉE'S REACTION
TO SHOCK

THE COMMUNAL COLD CURE

THE EXPANDO FIRESIDE SETTEE

NIGHT DUTY AT ONE OF THE FIRST RAILWAY SIGNALS

THE HYDRAULIC LAP

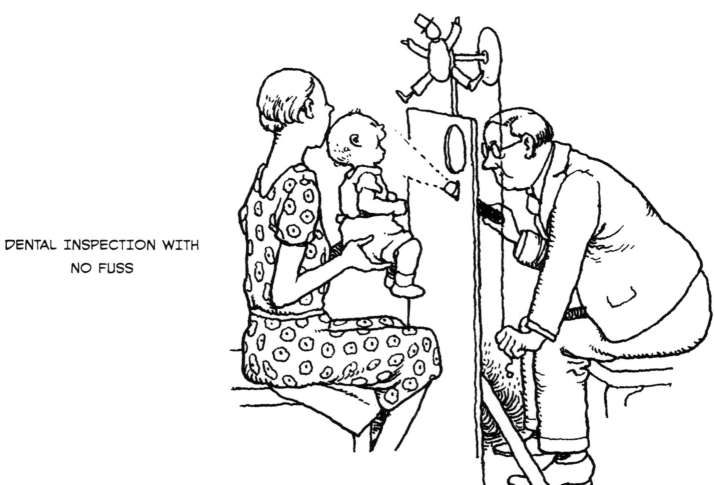

DENTAL INSPECTION WITH
NO FUSS

BUILDING THE FIRST LOCOMOTIVE

HOW TO COOK THE DINNER WHEN
MINDING THE BABY

QUICK ELECTRIC IRONING

THE CONVERSION OF AN OLD-FASHIONED
SCULLERY TO A BATHROOM

AN 'AIR FRAIS' BUNGALOW FOR WARM WEATHER

A NEARLY SUCCESSFUL EFFORT TO INTRODUCE THE ATMOSPHERE SYSTEM

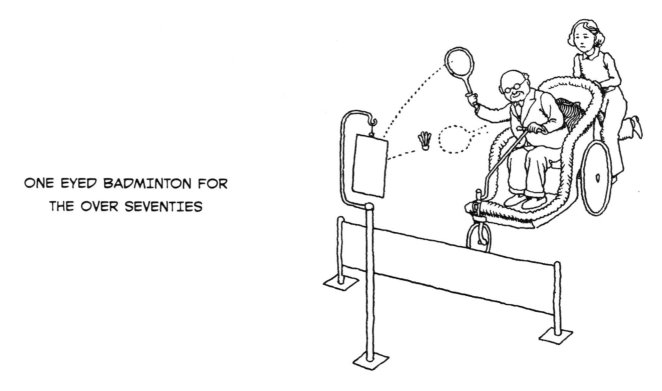

ONE EYED BADMINTON FOR
THE OVER SEVENTIES

TO INDUCE THE AFTER DINNER SNOOZE

THE COMPANY START STEAMER SERVICES

THE INFLUENZA CHAIR

HEATH ROBINSON

AN EARLY TYPE OF ENGINE FOR CLEANING TUNNELS

NEW USES FOR OLD RAILWAY ENGINES

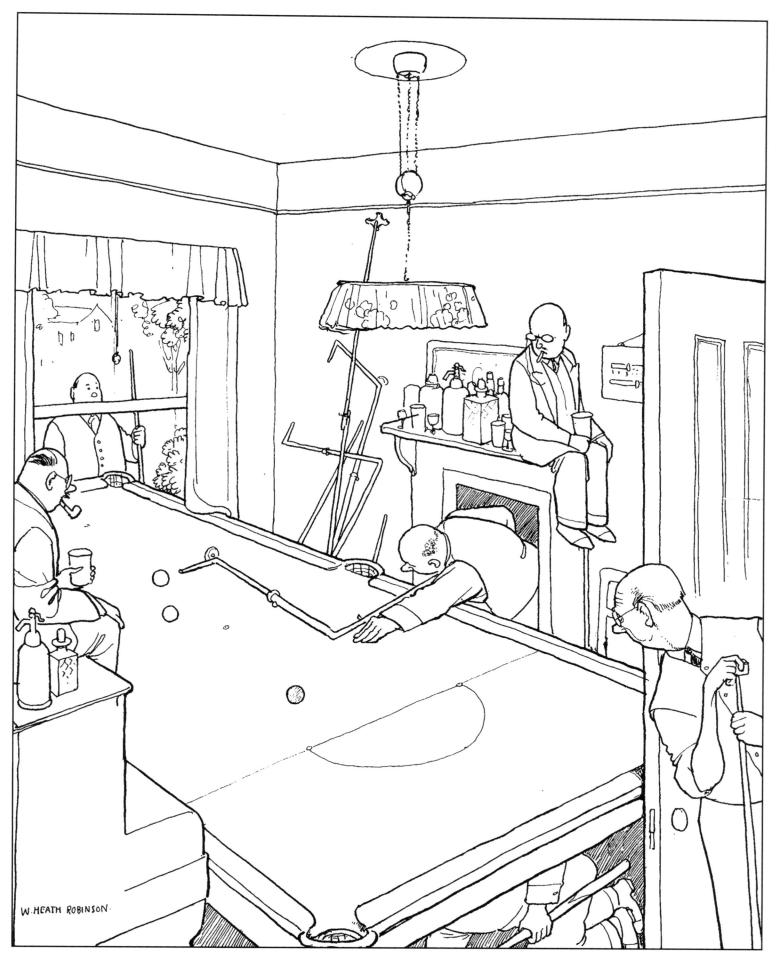

TAKING SEATS FOR THE FIRST LUNCH ON ONE OF THE FIRST TRAINS TO BE
EQUIPPED WITH RESTAURANT CARS

HOW TO DO WITHOUT
THE MANTELSHELF IN
A MODERN FLAT

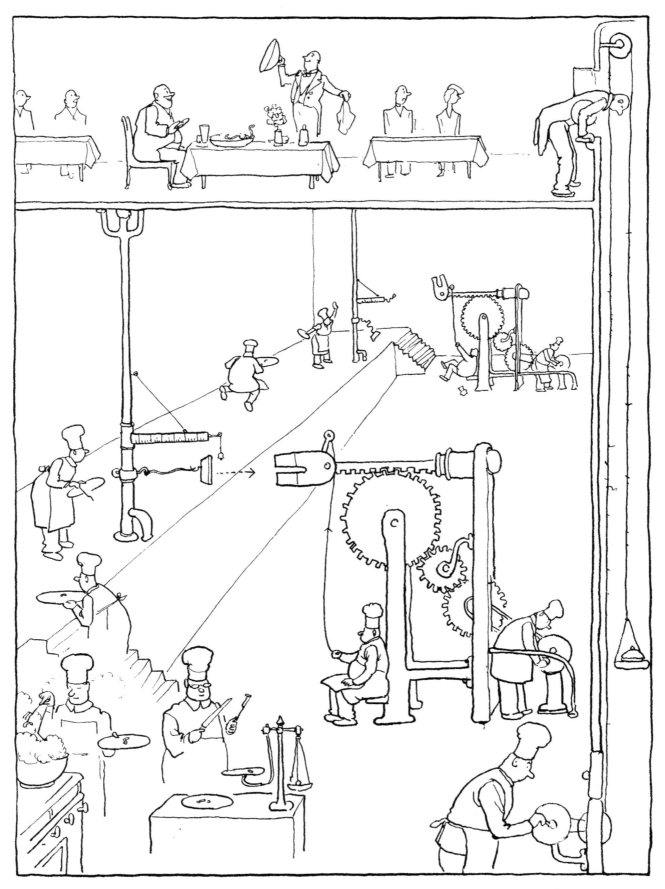

STRETCHING SPAGHETTI BY THE NEW MAGNETIC METHOD WHEN SPAGHETTI IS RATIONED

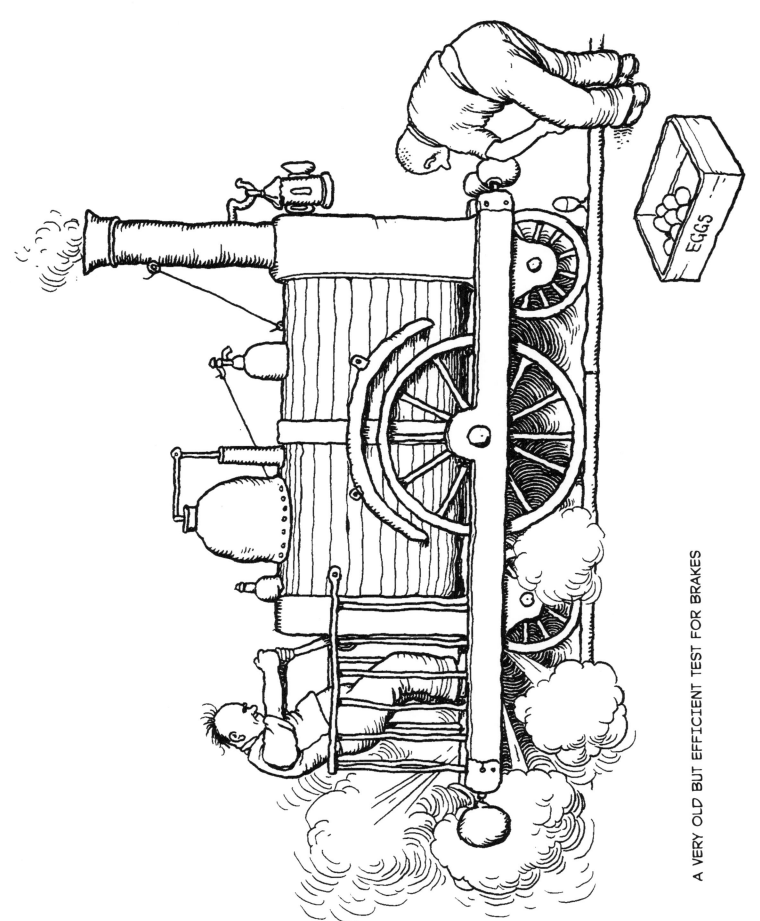

A VERY OLD BUT EFFICIENT TEST FOR BRAKES

YOU ARE THE LIGHT OF MY LIFE

I'LL FLY WITH THEE

LET US MEET BY MOONLIGHT

IF MUSIC BE THE FOOD OF LOVE --

(INNUENDO) A LITTLE BIT OFF THE TOP

MY HEART IS WHOLLY THINE

(COQUETRY) I AM EASILY CAUGHT

I AM YOURS FOR EVER

W. HEATH ROBINSON

125

ADJUSTABLE DOUBLE ENTRANCE TO A CONVERTED HOUSE